About Leaf Books

Our mission is to provide people with a pocket-sized read in the places where they are waiting, relaxing, taking a break. We aim to support writers by giving them a new market for their short stories and short non-fiction.

Don't forget to visit our website www.leafbooks.co.uk to tell us what you think of this book and to learn more about the writer and our other services.

Enjoy!

First published by Leaf Books Ltd in 2005
Copyright © Alexandra North

Leaf Books are proud to be working with
The University of Glamorgan

www.leafbooks.co.uk

Leaf
GTi Suite,
Valleys Innovation Centre,
Navigation Park,
Abercynon,
CF45 4SN

Printed by Inka
www.inkagroup.com

ISBN 1-905599-00-5
ISBN 978-1-905599-00-4

Adagio

by

Alexandra North

Alexandra North teaches in Cyprus. She completed her MPhil in Writing with the University of Glamorgan this summer having finished a collection of short stories and a novella entitled 'Running the Whiteboard', the latter being based on her experiences as a Moneybroker in London. She is now married and has a dog, a car and a garden.

Adagio

Laura put the car into first and rolled away. Helen, in the front passenger seat, rested her black suede handbag on her knees, pulled the seatbelt across and glanced over her right shoulder into the back.

'Hi, Thomas, you OK? Looking forward to it? I am. I've never been to anything posh like this before. I suppose you're used to it. Helen told me that you were really into this classical thing. And I've never been to Birchway Hall. Can't wait to see what it's like.'

His complexion seemed much darker than Laura's in the early evening light, Helen thought. They shared the same softly sloping nose and high cheekbones, but his jaw was not as square as his cousin's and his eyes were set much deeper. He was very attractive and she found herself opening the window an inch to cool the raspberry-red blotches she could feel radiating from her neck upwards. 'You don't mind me opening it, do you Laura?' She leaned forward to fiddle with the strap of her shoe and saw her friend shake her head.

Through the gap between the seats and their headrests Thomas tried to lip-read what Helen was saying, but she spoke too fast, tripping over words so that he couldn't make out the shapes of them. He drummed his fingers against his knees, waiting for her to remember to turn around and face him. This was only the fourth time they had met and it seemed that Helen still was not used to him being deaf.

A fine drizzle began to fall. Laura put the wipers on intermittent and flicked her sidelights on. As Helen twiddled with the straps of her burgundy velvet dress, adjusting and readjusting the length of them, she gabbled on about how she had burnt the cauliflower cheese, how the phone had rung whilst she was in the bath but she couldn't be bothered to move, how Zorro – her cat – flatly refused to come in when she had called. Laura, familiar with her friend's constant chitter-chatter, reacted in the right places, her eyes squinting as she scanned the road ahead. Thomas remained silent in the back, looking out the side window, watching the raindrops race down the glass.

'…and then I nearly ran out of the house without my ticket. Can you believe it? I know it's not really my scene, all this classical stuff, but Laura's raved on about it so much I'm actually looking forward to it. And I never miss an opportunity to buy a new outfit. Is that your own suit, Thomas, or have you hired it?'

Thomas did not say a word, just continued to watch the racing raindrops.

'You have to look at him, remember?' Laura reversed the car into a space in the car park outside Birchway Hall. 'Honestly, you should be used to it by now.' She put the handbrake on and switched the ignition off. She noticed Helen's face crinkle.

Helen looked over her shoulders at Thomas, peeping through the headrest. 'Sorry. I keep forgetting.'

'Don't worry about it.' His voice was slightly muffled. 'What were you saying?'

Helen watched his lips and saw how they

seemed out of sink with his slurring speech. 'Nothing, really. Just…I like your suit.'

She was suddenly at a loss for words. She cringed inside. Why did she always manage to make a fool of herself in front of him?

The three of them raced for cover as the drizzle became a heavy summer shower. A barrage of questions ricocheted around Helen's head but she said nothing.

The trio shimmied their way along their row, squeezing and bending past knees and shoes and handbags. Helen saw Thomas wave over to a man who was standing at the back of the Hall.

'Who's that?' She tapped Thomas on the arm. He turned to face her. She repeated the question.

'That's George Finch. I suppose you could say he's like a caretaker. He's looked after the place ever since I can remember. When I was younger, he'd let me in even though it was supposed to be locked up. He used to tell me about the history of the building or he'd tell me stories about the families that had lived here and which of them still haunted the Hall.' He laughed when he saw Helen quiver.

Once seated, Thomas remained perfectly still between the two fidgeting girls. The orchestra was in place: the men in black tuxedos with purple silk cummerbunds wrapped tightly about their waists, women in flowing black gowns with flashes of sparkle punctuating their ears and necks and wrists. Within a few minutes the mumbling audience hushed as the conductor and soloist entered and took centre stage.

'What's that instrument she's got?' Helen leant her head back behind Thomas and whispered to Laura.

'An oboe.'

'Not a clarinet?'

'No. This first piece is Marcello's Oboe Concerto. In D Minor. Trust me, it's an oboe.' Laura kept facing front.

'Oh.' Helen sat square in her seat. The main lights dimmed. She tilted her head back to her friend. 'I like her dress.'

'Sh. They're about to start.' Laura nodded

ahead.

'Sorry.' Helen fiddled with her programme, folding a corner in, plucking at the sharp edge. Another tilt of the head. 'Makes her hips stick out, though.'

'What?'

'The dress.'

'Helen!' Laura turned her head sharply and scowled.

'Mind, it's probably not too bad when she's sitting down.'

Laura tried to maintain the scowl but she could not stop the corners of her mouth lifting.

'Sh.' Thomas nudged both his elbows out to the sides jabbing each girl. The conductor raised his baton.

'What's he shushing at? He can't even… well, you know…'

Thomas tapped Helen's thigh with the back of his hand, still facing forward.

'I thought you couldn't…oh, never mind.' She sensed someone behind her leaning forward and heard them clearing their throat and letting out a long drawn-out huff. She turned to face the cougher. 'Sorry.' She shrank back into her seat and plucked at the programme. Thomas reached across and slowly pulled the card from her hands and placed it on the floor by his feet. The string section simultaneously raised their bows in preparation. Helen felt goose pimples race along her forearms and when the first steady down-bow, repeated six times, cried out from the violins, she shuddered.

The main lights once again illuminated Birchway Hall and excited murmurings filled the air. Thomas stood up and stretched his arms. Laura ferreted in her handbag for the car keys. Helen's focus was fixed on the empty stage, the arcs of metal chairs, the sheets of music perched on the stands. Thomas waved his hand before her face and she jumped, blinking hard. She looked about her and saw that the audience had dispersed, some still jamming the bottleneck of the main entrance.

'You've got a smear of black…' Thomas pointed to Helen's right eye.

She ran the side of her finger beneath her eyelid.

'No. In the corner.' He moved his hand towards her face, shied away, hesitated, moved forward again and gently wiped away the splodge of mascara. His hand felt cold. Refreshing.

'You been crying, you big girl?' Laura teased.

'No. No!'

The cousins looked at her with the same raised eyebrow expression.

'Well, you know what I'm like. I cry at anything these days. Adverts, even. Especially the RSPCA one they've got on Sky where they find the kitten in a dustbin and the dog with his ribcage sticking out, but then you see them all bandaged up and sitting on a comfy sofa and…'

'Oh, God. She's back with us. Well, we had a bit of peace for an hour. Come on, shake a leg, gobby.' Laura shooed her hands at Helen, motioning towards the main entrance which had cleared but for a few stragglers.

Outside, the showers had ceased. The night air was clean and fresh, sweet with the perfume of the lilac trees which lined the winding pathway to the car park.

'Coming back for coffee?' Laura checked her mirror and pulled away.

'I…er…' Helen tried to catch a glance of Thomas in the back, without making it seem as if she was looking at him at all. 'I…No, I don't think so.'

'Go on.'

'I'm not sure.' She caught Thomas' gaze. He winked at her. 'No.' She flicked her head sharply to the front. 'Could you drop me straight home?'

'You all right? It's still early by your standards. Can't tempt you?'

'I…I've got things to do, you know, in the morning. And Zorro will need letting in.'

'What's wrong with the cat flap?'

'Oh. Yes. Well, really, I've got heaps to do. Scrubbing the pan that contained my burnt offerings for a start.' Helen readjusted the strap of her dress.

'Surely the sacrificial cauliflower cheese can wait an hour or so?'

'There's other stuff as well.'

'You seem on edge. You sure you're OK? Come on, just a coffee. Or I'll be forced to tell Thomas about the time you peed yourself at Alton Towers.'

'You wouldn't!'

'In a cable car.' Laura angled her head and aimed the anecdote at the rear view mirror in which she could see her cousin looking back at her. 'With five other people.'

Thomas laughed. Loudly.

'You cow! I can't believe…OK. Just a coffee.' Helen folded her arms across her middle and stared into the wing mirror. She could not see Thomas, but she knew he was looking at her.

Helen curled her legs beneath her on Laura's two-seater sofa, hands clasped around a mug of coffee. Thomas sat on the floor, legs outstretched, his back leaning against the armchair, swilling his red wine clockwise in the bottom of his glass.

'I'm sorry, you guys.' Laura sighed. 'I'm going to have to bail. I'm knackered. Helen, you know where all the blankets are if you want the sofa for the night. Thomas has got the spare room.'

'Thanks. But I'll probably walk home in a bit. It's nice enough.'

'On your own?'

'I'm a big girl now.'

'I could walk her back.' Thomas gulped down the last mouthfuls of wine and put his glass back down on the grate of the fireplace.

Helen noticed that his voice was less muffled now. She wondered if she had imagined it earlier. Or was she used to it? She couldn't decide.

'Well, I'm off. No tricks, Thomas. Goodnight both.'

Thomas and Helen said goodnight to her and watched her shuffle sleepily out of the room, closing the door behind her.

'Tricks?' Helen looked at him through narrowed eyes.

'I don't know what she means.' He gave her

an impish smile, shrugging his shoulders. 'You two have known each other for years, haven't you?'

'Since Senior School.'

'She's always talking about you – "Helen did this" and "Helen did that". You seem close.'

'Like sisters, I suppose. I haven't got any real ones. We kind of adopted each other. She knows pretty much everything there is to know about me. What about you, though? Does she know everything about you, or is there some dark secret lurking?'

Thomas laughed. 'Sorry to disappoint. No, I'm afraid with me it's what you see is what you get.' He yawned, arching his back, extending his arms in front of him.

'Not such a bad thing sometimes.' She coiled some strands of hair around her fingers. 'Can I ask you something?'

'How could I hear the music?'

'Am I that see-through?'

'It's a fair question.' Thomas loosened his tie and pulled the loop over his head and unfastened the top button of his shirt.

'I'm just curious. And the last few times we've met, well, we've never really had the chance to talk about your being…'

He gave her his raised eyebrow expression again.

'Oh, God. That sounds crap, doesn't it?'

'You can say it, you know. Deaf. It's not a dirty word.'

'Sorry…So, I was wondering…why go to a concert if you're deaf? There, I've said it. I mean, I'm not totally stupid, I know about that percussionist, Evelyn whatsername…'

'Glenny. Evelyn Glenny.'

'That's it. She's the best in the world. And I can see how she does it, feeling the vibrations and that, but that's because she's in such close contact with the instruments. But to sit there, so far away. I just don't get it.' Helen laid her arm along the back of the sofa and rested her head against the cushion.

'I hear things in my own way. Sometimes I can feel it, taste it…'

'What? Taste? Don't wind me up.'

'I'm not.'

'That's just stupid. I mean, I know that you use your other senses more when you've lost one. I saw it on that SAS programme where they're tortured and stuff.'

Thomas threw his head back and laughed. She liked his teeth. Clean. Straight. 'I think there's a bit more to it than that. But I can see where you're coming from.' He muttered SAS under his breath and chuckled.

Helen pulled the fleecy throw over her legs and rested her empty coffee mug in her lap. 'Were you born deaf? Have you ever heard anything? An oboe, a baby crying, sirens, dogs barking, anything?' Helen buried her face in her hand and peeked through a gap in her fingers. 'I'm not very good at this, am I?'

'No. But I'll give you ten out of ten for effort.'

She threw the fleece over her head and stamped her feet on the sofa. When she reappeared her face was almost the colour of her burgundy dress. 'So, what happened? Were you born deaf? Have you had to learn to do this listening thing?'

'I could hear up to the age of seven. Not perfectly, but enough. I remember sounds I heard back then, but then I think, is it a true memory or am I imagining what the sounds must be like?'

'Confusing or what?'

'Not any more. Not really.'

'I just can't begin to imagine what it must be like.'

'It's probably me. I'm not that good at explaining it in words. Tell you what, you up for a late night walk?'

'Where to?'

'Come on. You'll see.' He jumped to his feet, holding his jacket out to put across Helen's shoulders. Warily, she slipped her arms into the sleeves. The lining felt cold and slippery against her skin.

She turned to face him. 'Why do I get the feeling you're up to no good?'

'Me? As if. Come on.' He grabbed her hand and yanked her out of the house at a half-running pace so that she stumbled on her heels. She let out a yelp. He turned and shushed her, pointing up the stairs.

'How the hell do you do that? You weren't even looking.' Helen looked at him in bemusement.

He cocked his head, winked and whisked her out of the front door.

They had been walking for almost half an hour before they smelt the familiar perfume of the lilac trees hanging in the air. The mugginess in the atmosphere had lifted since the rainstorms and though Helen appreciated the coolness she was glad to be wearing Thomas' jacket. She watched him as he walked eagerly in front of her, a bounce in his step, his energy contagious. She remembered how at the beginning of the evening he had seemed stuffy and uncomfortable in the back of the car. He was very different now. Relaxed, mischievous, bubbling. He began to run down the winding pathway to the Hall. She pulled his jacket closer and laughed as she joined him, clip-clopping down the path in her heels.

When she caught up with him she grabbed

his arm. 'You're not thinking of breaking in, are you?'

'Just stay here a sec.' Thomas disappeared from sight for what seemed forever to Helen and finally came back waving a key.

'Jesus!' She was whispering, she didn't know why. 'Where the hell have you been?' She looked at the key. 'And where did you get that? Christ! You didn't steal it, did you?'

'Don't be daft. There's a small type of outbuilding round the corner. George lives there. Remember? George Finch. I just asked if I could borrow the key to the main Hall for a while.' He unlocked the door and pushed it open.

As she tiptoed across the grey stone floor towards Thomas she could hear the clacking of her heels reverberating, bouncing off the walls until, finally, their echo was lost amidst the aged beams high in the roof.

It was gloomy. The light from the Victorian-style lamps which illuminated the pathway outside crept through the narrow windows and the stained glass feature window at the front of the Hall, behind the orchestra's chairs which were still laid out in their arcs. The audience chairs had been stacked to the side of the room in piles of six or seven and Thomas proceeded to drag two of them across the floor to the centre. He sat down and patted the chair beside him. Helen took her seat, her gaze firmly fixed on the haunting image depicted in the stained glass window of a woman, sat at a great pipe organ, her fingers resting over the keys.

'Who's that?' she asked, pointing at the window.

'Ah, that is Saint Cecilia. Patron saint of music. Look, she has two guardian angels watching over her. See how their eyes are raised, their mouths are open? They're singing their hearts to the heavens.'

'Why?'

'There are different legends surrounding her life. But she was a real woman back in the fifth century. From a young age she dedicated her life to God with a vow of chastity. But she was told that she had to marry…'

'Did George Finch tell you all this?'

'Don't knock him! He's a knowledgeable old bugger. Anyway…'

'She had to marry…'

'Yep. She had to marry, against her will, a young man called Valerian. One legend has it that on her wedding day, whilst music played, she sang her heart to God, praying for him to protect her virginity. And on their wedding night, when Valerian entered their room he saw angels. Some say that the angels told him that his brother would be killed if he, Valerian, slept with his new wife. Others say that he heard such beautiful music and saw her sadness so clearly that he was overcome and agreed to protect her chastity. Whichever, it seems that her prayers were answered. But, after two unsuccessful attempts to murder her, she was finally killed for her love of God.'

'That's terrible…She's beautiful, isn't she?' Helen whispered. The lemony glow from the lamps outside spilled through, breathing life into Cecilia. Helen couldn't believe she hadn't noticed the window earlier. For a split second, she thought she could hear a single soprano voice ringing above the lower harmonies of a female choir. She jolted as she felt Thomas' hand on top of hers.

'You OK? You look flushed.'

'I thought I could…did you…' she saw his puzzled expression, 'nothing, I'm fine. Thanks.'

Thomas shuffled his chair closer still until their arms and thighs were pressing together.

'So, what are we doing here?' She wriggled about in her chair, kicking her shoes off.

'I'll show you. OK. Now, close your eyes. No peeping.' He took hold of her hand and angled himself so he could see her mouth.

'You're not going to do something horrible to me, are you?'

'No, but you've got to trust me. Take it seriously or it won't work. Close your eyes.' He squeezed her hand.

'Sounds like a therapy session.' Helen lifted her chin and squinted through her half-closed eyes.

'Are you going to take this seriously?'

'Sorry, Thomas.' She sucked her lips in,

trying to stop herself from smiling.

'OK. Close your eyes. Breathe in through your nose, out through your mouth. Nice and steady.'

'Oh, we do this in Yoga.'

'Clear your mind.' His voice was stern for a second then immediately softened. 'Concentrate on your breathing. Let your muscles relax. Now, go back to when we pulled up outside the Hall earlier tonight. Feel the rain against your skin. Is it cold, warm, hard?'

'Soft. Cool.'

'Smell the freshness in the air and the lilac trees outside the entrance. Picture the Red Admiral perching on the clematis trailing up the wall. Watch the women dashing inside for cover and see their heels clicking on the gravel. When you sit down watch the people, their faces, their mouths, feel their excited whispers gently tickling at your skin.' Thomas brushed her cheek with the inside of his thumb. Helen tilted her head towards him, nuzzling against his thumb, urging him to continue, the same way Zorro rubbed against her calves.

'Smell the dusky perfume of the old woman in front, taste the shoe polish her husband has rubbed into his new brogues. The mutterings of the couple behind resonate through your body, making your shoulders ache, making your neck feel heavy. You look ahead and see the stained glass window at the end of the old Hall. Look at the light coming through it. It's not harsh daylight, but a dim streetlight, flickering through the drizzling rain, drifting like mist into the Hall, resting in the cracks and crevices, seeping through the floorboards. Watch how it breathes life into Saint Cecilia. See how the eyes of the angels change, become glassy, watery, alive.

'Feel the warmth tingling at your fingertips. The lanterns down the centre aisle make you feel safe, comfortable. At the end of the aisle, before the window, you see the orchestra. The conductor and the oboist walk in. The string section raise their bows. One note, repeated six times, slowly, at a walking pace. Hear it? Down, up, down, up, down, up. Watch the bows moving at slightly different angles to reach the harmony. See their left hands loosely holding the neck of the instrument, their wrists quickly but barely rocking back and fore to produce the vibrato. The soloist takes a deep breath but you hardly notice it. She moistens her lips and places the reed gently between them. Her shoulders rise, elbows widen.' Thomas traced the outline of Helen's mouth. The tickling sensation made her jerk away for a second, then she opened her mouth a little, letting his finger run between her lips. He placed her finger on to his wrist so that she could feel his pulse. 'The steadiness of the strings is like a heartbeat. Sure, continuous, subtle. How are you feeling?'

'Sad.'

'Why?'

'The oboist's face. She looks sad. Her eyes are closed, head tilted, eyebrows dipping ever so slightly. I can see her fingers letting go of the keys, from the bottom up, then she presses them back down, until all the silver pads are held in place…rising, falling.' Helen kept her eyes closed but felt Thomas' stare burning into her, not uncomfortably. She could feel his breath on the tip of her nose and in the corner of her right eye. His hand cupped the side of her face. Again, she nestled into it.

'There is a crescendo. How can you tell?'

'The violinists sit forward a little in their seats. Backs dead straight.'

'And the decrescendo?'

'They sit back.' The corner of Helen's mouth raised a fraction as she began to follow him completely, understand him.

'If this music could feel like something, what would it be?' His voice was soft and fluid.

'Like the softest blanket, feathers, wings, wrapped around me. Weightless. Safe.'

'What would it smell like?'

'Lilac trees.' She answered immediately.

'Look like?'

'Look like?' she repeated, giving herself time to think. 'Just like the window. Like Cecilia, sad at the thought of having to break her vow, singing her heart to the heavens, a woman, loving, being loved back.' Her speech was steady and clear. There was no tripping over words in her haste to get to the end of the sentence. Helen angled her head slightly away from Thomas. He could see another mark of black had formed beneath her eyelid. Without hesitation this time, he wiped it away.

'And taste?' He moved closer until his mouth was only centimetres from hers. As he exhaled Helen drew in his breath.

'Taste?' There was a faint hint of a smile in her voice. 'Salt water? No. Honey. Both.'

As he kissed her she felt goose pimples race along her forearm and in her mind she heard the first six strokes crying out from the violins.

For more information about Leaf Books and our services, please visit our website:

www.leafbooks.co.uk

- Complete List of Leaf Books
- Writers' Biographies
- Readers' Forum
- Ebooks
- Audio Books
- MP3 Downloadable Books
- Stockists
- How to Submit a Story to Leaf
- Competitions
- Writers' Services
- Jobs with Leaf

Competitions and Submissions

The Leaf competition and submission calendar enables us to gather stories, non-fiction, poetry written by new and established writers in the UK and abroad.

Every entry or submission is read by at least two members of our readers' panel. The panel consists of book and story lovers who represent a wide selection of backgrounds and tastes. We are very proud of this selection procedure and believe it gives a fair chance to every writer who sends us their work.

Leaf Competitions Entry Form

Name_____
Address_____
_____
_____
Email _____
Phone_____
Competition Title _____
See Website for details of Competitions and Closing dates.   www.leafbooks.co.uk
Title of Story/Piece/Poem
1._____
2._____
3._____
4._____
I enclose cheque, made payable to Leaf, for £_____ (£5.00 for each story, £2.50 for each poem, and £10 for each critique).
Please send entries to:
Leaf, Gti Suite, Valleys Innovation Centre Abercynon, CF45 4SN.